Ben and Annie

Ben and Annie

by Joan Tate

Illustrated by Judith Gwyn Brown

Doubleday & Company, Inc.

Garden City, New York

1974

ISBN : *0-385-08570-2 Trade*

0-385-08835-3 Prebound

Library of Congress Catalog Card Number 73–9048

Text Copyright © 1973 by Joan Tate

Illustrations Copyright © 1974 by Judith Gwyn Brown

All Rights Reserved

Printed in the United States of America

First Edition in the United States of America

U. S. 1812354

Ben and Annie

1

It's cold and wet, the rain slashing against the windows, the wind roaring in the chimneys, shaking the old house, whistling drafts under the doors. The apartments, all three of them, seem silent, because of the noise.

It's a good day for Ben to go straight home from school; no hanging about today. It's wet. And cold. And home and fire and food are the only things to think about.

Ben races up the stairs. The hall is dark, the tiles on the floor smudged with muddy footprints. He has crept past Annie's door so that he can surprise her. Then he races up the bare wooden stairs, fishes his key out and opens the door to his apartment. Mother's home, and there's a smell of cooking.

"That you, Ben?"

"Mm."

"What a day! Are your feet wet?"

"Mm."

"Bring your shoes in here and I'll put them by the stove. Find your slippers. The fire's on in here, but it's chilly."

Ben listens absent-mindedly, not really listening. Mother always says the same things. She's home early today. That always means the fire's on, which is good on wet, cold days. Their big living room is the best room in the house. They use it for eating in, and for cooking, and for sitting and talking and watching television. It's a good room and Ben always likes to come back to it, even when it's crowded with Mother, Dad, Sue back from her office, and him.

The house isn't built for apartments. It's an old house, once a rich man's mansion, perhaps, or so Ben likes to think. Now it's three apartments, Annie's downstairs, three big rooms, theirs in the middle, one big room and three smaller ones. And the young married couple at the top, only just come. Ben hardly knows them, just sees them on the stairs now and again. The conversion is a cheap job, Ben's dad says, hardboard wall partitioning off the stairs to make the apartments self-contained. But they have it to themselves, Mother keeps saying.

Ben takes his shoes off in the narrow little hallway and leaves them there. He pads into his room, the small back room which is his own. He has to sleep in the living room if Aunt Rachel comes to stay, but that's not often. It's his own. And the two water tanks for the bathroom are in there too, high up in the ceiling. He's used to the guggling, burbling noises they make.

And the tick-tock box is there, too.

Ben glances at it and gets his slippers out from under his bed. He goes back to the living room—they always call it the living room because Dad says that is where they live, where Mother does the cooking, where they squabble over the washing up; where there is the big table, the chairs around it, the armchairs around the fire and television and warmth.

"Put them down there," says Mother, pointing to the dark place down the side of the gas stove.

"They're soaking."

"They'll dry out there. If you put them in front of the fire, they'll crack. Are you wet?"

Mother grasps his shoulder and pats him all over his back, feeling.

"I had my raincoat on."

"All right. Don't want you down with a cold, now. Here, I've just made some tea. What a day! It's been dark all day."

Ben sits down at the table and drinks a cup of tea. Their meal will be at half-past five when the others get back. This is extra because Mother is back early. She doesn't work full time, but isn't always back before Ben, as she does her shopping on the way home. So sometimes it's Ben who makes the cup of tea for her. It's the only time they're alone together.

"Come on, drink it up now."

Ben slurps the hot tea inside him, gazing in a warm dream at the sworls and lines of the pattern on the formica top of the table. Dad fixed that—did it himself, noisily cutting it with a special saw and gluing it down with some strong-smelling adhesive that looked like sticky chewing gum well chewed. Ben remembers being made to sit on top of the table to keep it down while it stuck. It's easy to clean the top now.

He gets up from the table and puts the teacup in the sink.

"Thanks."

"You going to talk?"

"Mm."

"Bad day for her, today."

"Mm."

"Put your other sweater on if you're cold."

"I'm all right."

Ben slips across into his room and sits down on his bed. On the table wedged alongside it is the tick-tock box. That's their name for it. Dad calls it an intercom but that seems a dull name. Annie says it makes tick-tock noises if he fidgets with the microphone when he's talking. So it got called the tick-tock box. Or just the tick-tock.

Ben presses the switch and taps lightly on the grid of the mike.

"Tick-tick-tick," it goes.

There's a click.

"Thought you'd be back early today," says her voice, thin and hollow through the box. "But I didn't hear you. Did you get soaked?"

"Yes."

"The rain's been beating on this side of the house, so I haven't been able to see out even. Bashing on the glass, so I haven't been able to see out."

"What've you been doing?"

"Painting a picture."

"What of?"

"Well, at first it was going to be the view out of the window, but that wasn't much good today." There was a tinkling, tinny laugh. "So I tried painting a picture of my room. It's odd. Can't get things looking like they really do. The brush keeps sliding, too."

Ben laughs too.

"You've only had the paints a week."

"I know."

"Did Miss Turner come?"

"No, it wasn't her day. She comes tomorrow. I've supposed to have finished my book and done a picture of something from the book. But it's taken me all day, just trying to do a picture of the room."

"I can't draw at all."

"Can't you? Oh, I thought you might help.

Do a marvelous picture and then I'd tell Miss Turner I'd done it."

"You'd come out at the bottom of the class if you took mine."

The tinkling laugh again.

Ben snorts and suddenly the tank above his head begins to rumble.

"Can you hear my stomach rumbling?"

It's an old joke now, but it always makes her laugh.

"You must be hungry."

"Starving."

"What are you having for supper?"

Ben thinks.

"Roast hippopotamus with sparrow sauce. Pumpkin pie for dessert."

"Sounds good. D'you know what I'm having?"

"No."

Ben always says no, because if he said yes, he'd be spoiling the game.

"Whale steaks in gravy."

"And after?"

"I'll tell you later, when I've had it."

That means she hasn't been able to think

of anything. Cheating, thinks Ben. She's had all day to think of something.

"Cheating," he says.

A grating scraping rasping noise comes over on the box. It's Annie scraping her nails on the mike. She knows he hates it, that it sets his teeth on edge.

It all began as a sort of game, with two tin cans and string. The old pipes that had been used in the house before it was turned into apartments were still there and they ran right down through Ben's room into hers. Ben had run a long piece of string down the hole into Annie's room and fastened a can on each end of it. They had boomed down into the cans at each other, catching a few words now and again. A homemade telephone.

Then Dad had seen it and said:

"You two need a proper telephone."

They hadn't thought any more about it until one day Dad came back with a second-hand intercom. It had been taken out of an office and a modern one put in. And as Dad was a post-office engineer, getting it fixed up was a simple job.

That was three months ago.

Ben upstairs in his room.

Annie downstairs in her room, the room she hardly ever goes out of. Annie, who had come to live there with her parents a year ago. Annie, who is thirteen and two years older than Ben. But Ben is bigger.

"Is your mom home?"

"No, she went out to get something for supper about quarter of an hour ago. But Dad's here."

"Shall I come down?"

"After supper?"

"All right. Mother's home already, so I could be down at six or just after."

"What shall we do?"

"Checkers?"

"O.K.," says Ben.

Ben always wins at checkers, but Annie never seems to mind.

Ben hears Dad and Sue coming in together.

"They're all back now, so I'll be off to supper."

"All right, see you later."

"See you later, alligator."

There are two clicks and Ben puts the

16

small square mike back on the table. He gets up and goes into the living room.

"Hullo, Dad. Hullo, Sue."

"Hullo, Ben. Well, everyone here for once."

Mother gets dishes out of the oven and thumps them down on the table, which is already laid.

"The only good thing about this weather is that no one dawdles home in it," she says. "Come on, sit yourselves down and eat it while it's hot."

Dad washes his hands at the sink and sits down.

"I'm hungry."

"Me too," says Sue. "What a day!"

Then they're all sitting around the table, eating an ordinary supper, just like on any other ordinary day. And downstairs, Annie is having her supper, whale steak and gravy to make her big and strong, though it's probably soup and nothing will make her strong, ever.

"You going down tonight?" asks Mother.

"Mm," says Ben.

"What're you going to do tonight, then?" says Dad.

"Checkers."

"I saw a jigsaw puzzle in a shop window today," says Mother. "One of those old-fashioned ones—wooden—it was a map of some kind. Can Annie do jigsaws? It was second-hand, so not so expensive."

"I'll ask her," says Ben. "I've never seen one down there."

He goes into his room and clicks the switch.

"Do you like jigsaws?"

"Yes, but I don't do many. Too fiddly. Why?"

"Mother's seen one. Wooden pieces."

"Never tried one of those."

"I'll tell her. What did you have?"

"No whales."

"No?"

"No, just soup. But it was good. Are you coming down?"

"In a moment."

" 'Bye, then."

" 'Bye."

There's a click.

Ben goes back into the living room.

"She says she'd like to try," he says, sitting down to finish off his supper. "Your turn to do the washing up," he goes on to his sister.

"I did it yesterday," she says at once.

"You didn't, I did," says Ben.

Dad gets up to get his pipe and looks at the list pinned on the wall.

"Your turn, Sue. He's right," he says.

They take it in turns to do the washing up on weekdays. Dad's a great one for democracy, or so he says. It means a lot of talk and arguing, but things work out fair in the end. Ben goes downstairs.

2

Annie's mother lets Ben in and he goes straight to her room. It's a small room, next to their big kitchen. Annie has it to herself and everything in it is fixed up for her. She sits by the window in the daytime and her mother pushes her chair and the table over by the fire in the evening. Sometimes she gets pushed into the other room for the evening, depending on what's happening.

But when Ben comes, she's in her room.

They don't talk much, only on the tick-tock box. When Ben's there, they play checkers, or chess, or Monopoly or some other game. Monopoly is difficult, because Annie keeps dropping the money.

Tonight it's checkers, which Ben always wins. They can hear the television in the next room. Annie watches television a lot and likes

it. But she likes it best of all when Ben comes. He's real and he never gets tired of games.

"Last game," says Annie's mother, opening the door. "I must put Annie to bed now."

Annie's mother doesn't work, because she has to look after Annie all the time. A teacher comes twice a week and gives Annie lessons. And Annie listens to the radio, too. She's thirteen and reads a lot.

Ben has got so used to Annie that he doesn't notice any more that she's so small and thin and pale. She's just Annie, who lives downstairs and is on the other end of the tick-tock box. Ben has a plan, but he doesn't know how to carry it out. He doesn't say anything about it tonight because he's got to get the January gang to agree first. And he's got to get Annie's mother to agree too. He's not sure which is going to be the most difficult.

It's early spring and the weather's awful. But soon it will be better and the evenings will be longer and lighter. There won't be so much time for talking on the tick-tock box.

Ben wants the gang to take Annie with them.

The January gang is not really a gang. It's

a bunch of friends Ben has at school. They were all born in January, eleven years ago, and the four of them go to the same school. They're not really a gang, as four isn't a gang of people, and they haven't got a leader or anything like that. But Sue always talks about Ben and his "gang." They used to play together a lot, and now they're older they go farther away to play.

"Shall I take you down to the stores tomorrow?" Ben says to Annie, when her mother comes to put her to bed. Annie's bed is in her room, just like everything else Annie has.

On the last four Saturdays, Ben has taken Annie down to High Street on Saturday afternoon. By himself. They go to Woolworth's and Annie looks at everything and sometimes buys something. Sometimes they do some shopping for the two mothers. Now Ben's done it four times.

"Yes, please," says Annie. "I want some more of those colored pencils, for schoolwork. Can I, Mom?"

Annie's mother frowns and then says yes. She doesn't really like Annie out of her sight.

She's afraid. She's afraid Annie will be hurt or something will happen to her when she's not looking. But she likes Ben and is pleased Annie sees someone else sometimes. And it gives her a break. So she says yes and it's fixed.

Ben goes upstairs.

Next week he'll have to talk it over with the gang. The Easter holidays will be here soon and they'll want to go to the Slags as soon as it's nice enough. If Annie . . .

Ben goes off to sleep thinking about what he's going to say to the others. It won't be easy. John and Stan will be all right, he thinks. But Steve won't like it. If there's a boss in their gang, it's Steve, and he often gets his way. He's bigger than them all, which makes a difference. And he doesn't like girls at all.

Next day it's Saturday and it's stopped raining. That's good because Annie's mother always says no if it's raining, because Annie mustn't get wet. So after lunch, Ben goes downstairs.

Annie's mother is fussing around her chair, wrapping a rug around Annie's thin legs, fastening a woolly fur hood under her chin, putting a huge scarf around her neck and making sure she's got her gloves on. All Ben can see of Annie is her small white face and her pale blue eyes. They're smiling.

"Mom, you're strangling me."

"I'm not."

"Not too tight. It's always boiling in Wooly's."

"Ben can loosen it for you when you get there."

"One day I'll melt away," says Annie, "and Ben'll come back with a grease spot and no me."

"Don't talk like that," says her mother, and bends down to kiss her, as if she was going away for several years. "Come along, Ben, I'll help you down the steps."

Annie's mother takes the handle and pushes the chair out into the tiled hall. Ben opens the big front door and then catches hold of the footrest of the chair. Together they lift the chair down the four stone steps onto the pavement. It's an ordinary wheel chair, a light one of steel, not the kind with big wheels at the side, since Annie's not strong enough to push herself around any longer.

They set off down the street, Ben turning to wave to Annie's mother, who is standing on the steps watching them go. She always does that, so when they get to the corner, Ben swings the chair around and Annie can wave too. Then he swings it back again and they head for High Street.

Woolworth's is the best store for them because it's a new one and there's lots of room. Ben stumps along the road, saying nothing. Annie says nothing too, but looks and looks at everything that's going on. Everyone's out shopping on this fine Saturday, so there are lots of people in the street. When they get to Woolworth's, Ben pushes the chair up to one of the glass doors and shouts:

"Make way for the Queen!"

Someone always opens the door for him, then. And Annie says, "Thank you" very politely, with a little wave of her hand, and then she and Ben look at each other and laugh. The first time, Ben had had to struggle with the door, holding on to the handle of the chair with one hand and trying to push the chair through with the other. It was difficult because the doors were heavy and stiff. Then he tried the other way—just shouting something comical or silly. It worked like a dream and it made Annie laugh. Each time he had to think up something different. The first time he had said, "Watch your backs there, please" very loudly, and the whole crowd had turned around and someone had soon opened the door. The next time he'd shouted, "All aboard the Orient Express," and the same thing had happened.

"Make way for the Queen!"

A woman hears and turns around. When she sees Ben and Annie trying to get through the door, she holds it open.

"Thank you," says Annie as they sweep in.

"That's quite all right, dear. It's a pleasure," says the woman, and she smiles at Ben in that way that people have of smiling when they feel sorry for someone. Sickly. Ben smiles back, because she did open the door, but he grinds his teeth too, and wishes people wouldn't feel sorry for Annie, because she hates it.

"Pencils," says Annie, and they move over

to the stationery counter. Out in the street Ben holds on to the handle all the time, because he's promised to. But in Woolworth's he has to let go sometimes because Annie can't see the things on the counters. She can see the ones on the lower shelves, but the higher ones she has to ask Ben to show her.

Today she buys colored pencils, made in Japan, which are really tubes of colored ink that look like pencils. They're rather expensive, but Annie can hold them well and her mother has given her the money for them. She has enough money over for a new drawing pad.

Then they go on a tour of the store and Ben suggests going downstairs today. That means the elevator, which isn't meant for customers. But Ben knows what to do.

He goes up to a supervisor.

"Will you take us down in the elevator, please?"

The supervisor nods—he's met Ben and Annie before—and he takes a straight key out of his pocket and opens the elevator doors. Ben wheels Annie in and the supervisor gets in with them.

Down they go, and Annie laughs again.

"My stomach's floating away," she says. "Catch it, Ben."

Ben swats the air with one hand and catches something that is nothing about four inches away from Annie's nose. "Your stomach, Your Majesty, with the compliments of the season," he says.

"Thanks so terribly much," says Annie in a silly voice, and they laugh again.

The supervisor grins and lets them out on the basement floor.

They go straight to the self-service cafeteria. Ben wheels Annie along the passage next to the counter, chanting out what it says on the labels. Annie doesn't eat anything here, but she likes to pretend she's ordering everything. Ben takes a bun and two fizzy orange drinks. He puts the tray on Annie's lap, says, "Hold tight" and wheels off toward a table. He takes the tray and sits down.

Annie sits and waits. Then Ben takes off her gloves and scarf and places the bottle of orange in her two hands. Annie can just hold it and she drinks slowly through the straw. Ben drinks his slowly too, so that he hasn't finished long before Annie has. She watches the people coming and going and Ben watches her.

Annie is so small. She's much smaller than Ben, although she is thirteen, and she's been ill all her life. Sometimes she has to go back into the hospital, but mostly she lives at home, never getting better. She used to be able to hold things easily, but now she can't. Ben doesn't give her any of his bun, because he knows she doesn't like taking it. Her mother feeds her at home and when she's out she likes to be like everyone else. Her hair is very fair, thin and silky under her hood.

"Home, now," says Ben, glancing up at the clock. It's taken them most of the afternoon and he knows Annie's mother fusses if they get late.

Gloves on, scarf done up, back to the elevator, call the supervisor, whoops, and they're up on the street level again. Up to the big glass doors and . . .

"Where's the doorkeeper?" roars Ben, looking fierce.

A man turns around to see who is being so cheeky, and then he sees it's Ben and Annie

and he opens the door wide for them, his frown vanishing off his face like magic. Ben bows to him as they go through.

"Thank you," says Annie, and when they are out on the street she laughs, the same tinkling laugh that Ben hears over the tick-tock, only not so tinny.

"Ben, you're always making me laugh," she says.

Ben gives the chair a jerk and walks faster. Annie's cheeks are quite pink and her eyes are bright. The parcel is down the side of the chair and when they get back to their street, there's Annie's mother waiting on the steps. She's been looking out for them through her front window, waiting for them, Ben knows.

Up the steps, in through the apartment door.

" 'Bye, Ben."

" 'Bye, Annie. I'll call down tomorrow morning."

"O.K."

Ben walks upstairs to his own apartment. He's sick of Woolworth's but he doesn't say so. Perhaps the gang . . . he'll have to talk it over with them.

3

Ben has seen a long time ago that Annie doesn't get much fun. And she likes fun. She's got lots of things and her mother and father buy her things to do as she sits there all day, often by herself or with just her mother. But she's a laughy person, and so's Ben. She likes excitement and crowds and movement.

Ben and Steve and John and Stan have three places where they play. The nearest is the street adventure playground in their area, where you can climb about and bang nails into wood and sass the leader and yell as loudly as you like. The next nearest is the park, but that's quite a way across the city. And the third's the Slags. That's much farther away and their favorite place. The Slags, as they are always called, were once slag heaps, but they've planted some kind of tough grass on them and it's the best place of all.

The weather takes a turn for the good at the end of the term and Ben starts mentioning his plan.

"There's a girl in a wheel chair down below at my place," he says, quite casually one day, when they're sitting on the bike rack at school, not doing anything in particular. "Thought I'd bring her along to the park next week."

"A girl!"

Just as Ben expects, Steve is all bristles. "We don't want girls with us."

"What do you mean, in a wheel chair?" says Stan. "Can't she walk?"

"No," says Ben.

"Do you have to push her?"

"Yes," says Ben.

"Like a baby buggy!" Steve sounds scornful. "You're not catching *me* pushing buggies around."

"She could just watch us," Ben says. Ben's really obstinate once he gets something into his head. "How'd *you* like to be in a chair all the time?"

That silences them.

"But we only mess around," says John feebly.

"She can watch. There's lots of things going on in the park."

"My granddad's in a wheel chair," Stan says suddenly. "He likes to sit out in the street. He says he sees the world that way."

"What's her name?" says Steve, looking grumpier than ever, because he can hear the others are interested.

"Annie."

"Annie-pannie! Poof! What a name," says Steve.

"What's wrong with Annie?" says John. "My sister's name is Anne, and they often call her Annie."

"I'd rather be called Annie than Stevie," says Stan, suddenly brave, as he's usually the one who says nothing and falls in with everything.

Steve leaps on Stan and in a flash they're a tangled mess of arms and legs on the ground.

When they're untangled, Ben says again:

"I'll bring her next week, then, shall I? On Wednesday. Will you bring the ball, Stan?"

Stan nods.

"I'm not coming," says Steve.

There's a silence.

"O.K.," says Ben.

They walk away stiffly, still together, but no one saying a thing. They've been together for a long time and they don't mean it, but they've said it. Ben's said he doesn't mind if Steve isn't there and Steve hasn't said anything. They've arranged to meet at the park if it's fine on the first day of the holidays. Afternoon. With the soccer ball. Somewhere near the swings.

Ben goes off home and John walks with him for a short while, as he lives in the same direction.

"Is she sick, this girl?"

"Sort of."

"What sort of?"

"Well, she's sick all the time, not just sick one week and better the next. She lives in the apartment below and I talk to her on my intercom."

"Your what?"

Ben explains to dim old John, who listens as if he was being told a Wild West story. John plans to start saving up for an intercom himself. But who is he going to talk to on it?

John goes off down his street and Ben goes home. He opens the front door and stumps loudly down the hall and up the stairs. He gets his key out and knows at once there's no one at home the moment he opens the door.

The tick-tock box is ticking away like mad when he gets to his room.

"You don't have to stamp in like that," says the voice. "I can hear you if you walk ordinarily."

"Do you want to come to the park with us on Wednesday?" says Ben.

"What? The park?"

"Yes."

"To do what?"

"Play soccer with the gang."

"Is that where you play?"

"Yes."

"And I can come too?"

"If your mom lets you. You can be referee."

Annie giggles.

"I don't know the rules."

"You can make them up."

"You could tell me them. I've watched often enough on TV."

"You can hold our jackets, too."

"But what about Mom?"

Ben is silent for a moment.

"Shall I get Dad to ask her?" he says. "He might."

Annie says nothing for a while. Then she says in a small voice:

"It'd be better if you asked. Mom likes you."

"Doesn't she like my dad?"

"She's only spoken to him that once, when he came to put the tick-tock in."

"O.K. I'll ask. When? This evening?"

"I'll call back."

"O.K. After supper? Yes?"

"Yes."

"Alligator."

"Big potater."

"Bing."

"Bong."

"Bang!"

They switch off at exactly the same moment. Ben goes into the living room and makes a pot of tea and then Mother comes in and dumps the shopping on the table.

"That's just what I need," she says and sits down as soon as she's got her coat off.

After tea, Ben goes into his room and waits.

Tick-tick-tick.

"Yes?"

"Better come tomorrow."

"Why?"

"It's not a good moment tonight," says Annie.

"All right."

"'Night."

"Mind they don't bite."

"You're a fright."

"Alligator."

"Big potater."

"Bing."

"Bang."

"Bong!"

Annie's giggles come over the line just before he switches off.

Next day is a better moment to ask, though Ben doesn't know why. He goes down and he asks if Annie can come with him to the park on Wednesday, if it's fine.

43

Annie's mother looks anxious.

"She's never been that far with you. Suppose it rains?"

"If it rains, we won't be going."

"Supposing it rains while you're there?"

"We could take the umbrella."

That's an umbrella they have so that Annie doesn't get wet if there's a shower.

"I suppose you could."

"I'll make sure she's all right."

"I know, Ben, but—"

"Mom, I'd like to go," says Annie suddenly. She hasn't said anything up till then, but now she looks at her mother. "It's ages since I was in a park. And Ben knows how to manage the chair."

"I could come with you," says her mother.

Ben looks down at his feet and Annie says nothing. That isn't at all the same thing and Ben doesn't want to go to the park with Annie's mother. The gang would never speak to him again. Somehow Annie's mother seems to know something's wrong.

"I couldn't manage that far, now, could I?" she says. "All right. But you'll be very careful, won't you, Ben?"

Ben nods. Of course, he's always careful, isn't he? How could you be anything else?

So it's settled. All they have to do now is to hope for fine weather. They need some, as it seems to have been raining for weeks on end. But Annie needs it too.

4

The jigsaw puzzle is a success. It's an old one, as Ben's mother had said, and was in one of those shops which are crammed with all sorts of things that aren't new. The jigsaw's made of wood, the pieces quite big, so Annie can put them together quite easily. It takes up several days, off and on, and when it's finished it's a map of the world with the British Empire in red.

"Look," says Annie. "Mom says it must be years old, because it's got India and Canada in red. And lots of Africa, and I know that's wrong."

"Did you do it all yourself?"

"Yes," says Annie. "And Dad says I should try and do it upside down now. With no picture to help."

"Did you try?"

"Yes, but it was no fun."

"School finishes tomorrow," says Ben. "And it's fine out."

They don't say any more, but they know what the other is thinking.

On Wednesday, the tick-tock box is busy.

"Are you ready?"

"Not yet."

"I'm on my way."

Annie's voice squeals down the wire.

"No, wait!"

"O.K. I might."

"Come in ten minutes."

"Eight."

"Wait."

"Batter."

"Chatter . . . oh, I can't think of anything today . . . gillie-pilly."

"Ah . . . you're silly."

"Ping."

"Pong."

"Plunk."

Annie's plunk comes a second after Ben's and they both laugh.

Annie is wrapped up warm, the umbrella

tucked in under the chair. Annie's mother flaps around, but at last they're off.

"Be back before half-past four," she says, as they set off down the street.

They wave and Ben feels like running. The sun is out and there's no wind. He pushes the chair along, easing it down over the curbs, tipping it back a little as he does so, and all the way to the park, they say nothing at all, but sometimes above the noise of the traffic, Ben can just hear Annie singing quietly to herself.

He heads for the swings down in the far corner. That's where they are to meet and that's where most goes on. The small kids come in droves to have a swing and the older ones take rides on the merry-go-round and zoom down the slides. Ben likes the swings too, but there are too many kids on them these days. He sees John a long way away.

"This is Annie," he says, when they get up to John. "Where's the others?"

"Stan's coming—he's just dumping his kid brother in the sand box."

John stares at Annie a bit until Ben nudges him, quite hard.

"What about Steve?"

"Dunno, but there's others here who'd like a game."

They hang about for a while and soon there are about eight or nine of them. But no Steve. Stan's brought the ball, a white plastic one he had for Christmas. They start kicking it around.

"Let's start," says Ben, though he's disappointed Steve hasn't come. He thinks it's his fault, and for a moment he wishes he hadn't brought Annie. He looks across at her sitting there in the sun. She's not looking at him, but all around the park and she looks happy.

He goes over to her and puts his jacket on the arm of her chair.

"Here you are, referee," he says. "We haven't got a whistle, so you'll just have to hang on to the jackets."

The others come up and cluster around the chair, putting jackets and sweaters all over it, hanging them on armrests, across the handle, on the footrest, on the wheels.

"You look like an old-clothes man," says Stan, and the others laugh and then they rush off. Two sweaters, one jacket and a

duffle bag are the goal posts and they all know Annie is watching.

"She watches a lot of soccer on TV," Ben has said, "so no fouling and everyone's got to be as good as Pele."

Ben's got the ball and is dribbling it toward his goal, when suddenly someone swoops in from nowhere and steals the ball from him and rushes off with it toward the other goal. It's Steve.

Ben watches him tear down the grass, nipping in and out between the others and then he shoots hard at the goal, and the goalie, who is John, hasn't a chance. Ben says nothing, and they start again from the middle, Ben center forward on one side, Steve on the other, the boy who had been center forward moving back one for Steve.

No one says anything and Ben has seen that Annie is watching their game. There are other games and there are all the people on the swings and slides to watch, but she's watching their game and waving when there's a goal, no matter what side gets the goal.

When they stop, they go over to Annie's chair to get their jackets and sweaters. Everyone's hot and puffing and they grab their sweaters and jackets and put them on or pull them over their heads. Steve picks his up from the grass some way away and comes ambling over.

Ben thinks he ought to say something, but doesn't know what. He wants Steve to know he's pleased Steve has come, but he's not going to make it seem that they can't do without him. Then Annie speaks.

"You play well," she says, looking straight at Steve. He looks confused and stares down at his shoes. The others all grin and at once start telling Annie.

"He's our best player."

"Plays on the junior team."

"Everyone's interested in him."

"He'll be a pro one day."

Ben feels a bit jealous, but at the same time it looks as if Steve is not going to leave the gang, so he says nothing.

"Want a swing, Annie?" says Steve, casually.

At once, Ben is worried. He knows Annie can't hold the chains, not without help, and he doesn't want her to get out of her chair.

He has hardly ever seen her out of her chair and knows she can't get out of it by herself.

"We must get back," he says quickly.

"Ah, just one," says Steve. "We'll hold on."

Annie looks up at Ben. She would like a swing, but can't see how she could have one.

"Next time," she says, quickly too. "Next time. My mom gets worried if I'm home late."

Ben is relieved.

"Come on, then," he says, and turns the chair around. Stan and John help push the chair up the slope and Steve walks behind.

"Tomorrow, same time, same place," Steve shouts, as they go off in different directions.

"O.K."

Annie waves.

They get back in time and there's no trouble. After supper, the tick-tock box ticks and Ben switches on.

"That was fun," says Annie. "Did they mind?"

"What d'you mean?"

"Did the others mind I was there?"

"Of course not."

"But they didn't like the idea at first, did they?"

"Oh, well . . ."

"Thought so. Wish I was a boy."

"Why?"

"It's easier."

"They showed off today, because you were there."

"Did they?"

"Especially Steve."

"Is he one of your gang?"

"Mm."

"He's nice."

Ben feels jealous again, but he says nothing.

All that week, he takes Annie to the park to watch their games. The fresh air is good for her, and soon all the boys accept her sitting there, watching, like a kid brother. She talks about their game too, and they can see she's no fool.

They even give her a swing. Ben's told them that she has to stay in her chair, so they think up a plan which is safe and means she doesn't have to get out of it. It's Steve who has the idea.

One day they bring a strong wide board with them and fasten it on to one of the swings. Then, very carefully, they lift up

Annie's chair and sit the whole thing, Annie and all, on the board, the wheels hanging below it. Then Ben stands on one side and Steve on the other. They hold the chain to the armrests of Annie's steel chair. Then they swing her. She's got a belt right around her to keep her still in the chair. Of course, she can't go very high, but by standing each side like that, and moving with the swing, they can give Annie a gentle swing in the warm spring air.

Annie squeals with delight. She laughs and

shows her small white teeth and they laugh too, and as the swing falls back, she clings to the armrests and squeals as if she were racing through the air.

They don't tell Annie's mother, because Ben thinks she will put a stop to it, and the gang really like doing things for Annie, now, and there's quite a fight to push her up the slope to the park gates at the end of the afternoon.

But Ben tells his dad.

At first Dad looks alarmed.

"But we hold on to the chair and we never swing it high," says Ben. "Really we don't. Just like you swing a tiny kid who can't hang on properly."

"Well, you be careful," Dad says. "That's their only child and she's precious."

"But she *loves* it," says Ben, thinking about Annie's face and her thin fair hair floating about in the air. How *can* he explain to them?

"I bet she does," says Dad. "I bet she does. I bet it's the greatest fun she has, poor little devil."

"She's *not* poor," shouts Ben suddenly. "She hates people to think like that."

"All right, all right, son," says Dad. "I didn't mean anything. She's a lucky kid, with you carting her about."

Ben goes into his room. His plan's come off. He can go to the park and play with the gang and he can give Annie some fun too. It's fun seeing Annie having fun. It's great to think that it's him, Ben, who's done it all. And even Steve's still coming, too. Ben feels pleased with himself.

"Is that Matt Busby speaking?"

"It is." Annie giggles when she says it.

"How was the game today?"

"Well, Pele is shaping up nicely. Might make a player out of him some day."

"Yes, just what I thought."

"But the swing's the best, always," says Annie.

"Is it?"

"Yes. Like a bird on a clothesline."

"How do you know what a bird on a clothesline feels?"

"I just know."

"See you tomorrow, then."

"Yes . . . um . . . cracker."

"Jacker."

"Hunky."

"Dory."

"Jim."

"Jam."

"Jom!"

Ben's running out of ideas for switching off the tick-tock box. They've both got so good at it now, it's almost routine and it doesn't sound such fun as it did when they were inventing them, trying to get them off fast each time.

5

Annie goes into the hospital the next week, for her usual checkup. Ben and the gang decide to go to the Slags and see how things are there.

It takes half an hour to get to the Slags if you walk, five minutes on the bus. The Slags are in the old factory district where there used to be a whole lot of factories and foundries, most of which have gone now or are derelict. But the Slags have been left.

If you half close your eyes and look at the Slags, they seem like rolling green mountains, only small. They are rounded heaps of slag and the coarse grass that grows on them now makes them green. They've even planted a few trees here and there, which are taking a long time to grow, but they've survived, most of them.

There are dips and hillocks and hollow places; there are smooth crags and swooping hump-backed places. There's a steep bit and the rounded peak, right at the top, from where you can see for miles and miles, even if all you can see are buildings and chimneys and smoke. It's wild and there's lots of space and the best thing in the world is a metal tray.

Their two metal trays are both ancient and battered. They are hard to find and Ben and Steve guard them as if they were made of solid gold. They're big old enameled trays, chipped and scratched, which they got off a scrap heap. You can race down a grass slope on them at a stunning speed.

Ben and Steve have got clever at it. If you start fairly high up the highest slope, and you steer a bit, you can swerve at the bottom and get yourself right around the edge of that mound and then on down the next slope, which swoops you up to a stop on the other side. That's what they all try to do.

Sometimes they come off on the first curve and roll and roll down into the dip, the tray whizzing on by itself. Sometimes the tray tips or hits a bump and in a flash you're head over heels down the slope ahead of it and it comes racing at you at full speed and you have to roll out of its way before it hits you.

Ben and Steve own the trays, but they share them when they go to the Slags.

"What about a twin run," says Steve.

"O.K.," says Ben.

They take one tray and climb up to the ledge that is almost on the peak. They *sit* on the tray when there are two of them, since there's not room for two lying down. Ben in front and Steve behind. Then Steve pushes off and the tray starts fast down the straight slope. At the bottom there's a curve to the right and Ben and Steve have to hold tight and lean right over to the right, just the right amount, so that they don't tip the tray over when they get around the next corner. The tray slows a bit and swoops up over a small hillock, just tips over the top and then— swoosh—they're off down the next run. By now they're going really fast, the wind whistling past their ears and the dust from the grass blowing up into their faces. Right at the bottom of the run, there's a dip and then an upward slope slows you down and stops you. When you're two on the tray, you come down very fast and can get tipped off at the bottom, but Ben and Steve lean right back and haul the front of the tray up, just an inch off the ground, and—swoosh—up they go and slowly come to a stop where the others are waiting.

Today they've stuck on to the tray all the way and that doesn't happen often, so they're feeling good. Stan and John say they're going to try this time and off they go, trudging up to the top. But they only get halfway down the first slope and they can't get the tray to turn right around the bend, so off they come, and go rolling head over heels down into the dip. The tray is miles away and Ben races after it, laughing at the heap that is John and Stan, now struggling to their feet.

Ben and Steve are competing on the ski jump today. That's the most difficult of all. That's the straight slope down, then the slight slope up and at the end of the upward slope, you fly straight out into the air about two feet off the ground. That's where you come to grief. If you don't keep the tray flat, you're soon in a mess on the ground. But if you can keep it flat, you sail along through the air for a few yards and then land like a glider on the grass and scoot along to a stop.

The conditions today are perfect as the grass is dry and dusty, so the going's fast.

"Bet you I can do it today," says Ben, and sets off.

Down he goes, the tray hissing on the grass, up the small slope and wheeeeee, he's in the air and coming down. But the tray hits the grass crookedly and Ben's off, tumbling helter-skelter down the side of the down slope. Steve tries.

Hissssssss goes the tray on the grass, zoom up the slope, wheeeeee through the air and splat! The tray's down and Steve's hanging on for dear life, scooting along the grass at a great rate. At the last moment, the tray hits a bump and tips him off. So that one doesn't count.

They try several times, but neither has any luck today. Then they pack up and start off home, Steve carrying one tray, Ben the other.

The enamel is almost worn completely off the bottom of their trays, worn away by the grass and grit.

"Annie is home today," Ben tells Steve.

"Bring her along. Bet she's never seen anything like it," says Steve.

"It's an idea," says Ben.

It *is* an idea. Ben's been racking his brains to think up something new to show Annie when she gets back. The park's getting boring and is very full of people now, so there's hardly any room for soccer. Anyhow, it's getting too hot to play sometimes.

He switches on the tick-tock box when he gets back.

"Hi, stranger."

"Hullo, Ben. You coming down?"

"Later. What did they say?"

"Doctor says I'm looking better. Says it's all that fresh air."

"That's great."

"I told him about the park."

"What did he say?"

"Says that's why I'm better."

"I'll show you something even better tomorrow."

"What?"

"Can't tell you."

"Oh, come on."

"No, it's a secret," says Ben.

"I've thought up a new way of switching off—while I was in the hospital."

"What?"

"I say—*gallopy-pallogy*—and you say—*gutsy-goo*—and I say *liggamy-gillamy*—and you say *How*—and I say *are* and we both say *YOU* and switch off."

"Gallopy-pallogy."

"Gutsy-goo."

"Liggamy-gillamy."

"How."

"Are."

"YOU!"

They try it out and it works but it isn't all that good.

"It's gobbledygook," says Ben.

"It's what?"

"It's gobbledygook—words that don't mean anything."

"Gobbledygook, gobbledygook," says Annie. "See you later, alligator."

" 'Bye."

So next day they take Annie to the Slags to watch.

Annie watches, her eyes popping as the two of them swoop about on their old metal trays. Steve is showing off like mad and is wildly successful today, leaning this way and that and never coming off.

"I'd love to do that," says Annie to Ben, who is standing watching too.

"It's difficult," says Ben.

Steve comes panting up, grinning all over his face and dragging the tray behind him. He throws himself down on the grass and lies there, puffing.

"You see what a place it is, Annie," he says.

"I never heard of it before," says Annie.

"We found it last year," says Steve. "It's been left like this on purpose, a place to play, see?"

"Do you all come here?" says Annie, as only Ben and Steve have come today, taking it in turns to push Annie's chair on the way.

"Only the gang, though there's lots of other people who come here," says Ben. "Gets quite dangerous if there's too many."

"I've never done such a thing," says Annie again. "Wish I could."

Steve gets up and takes hold of the handle of the chair.

"I'll give you a little run on the slope," he says.

Ben jumps up and says, "No, I will."

Steve struggles for a bit, but then he gives way.

"Let's both; it's safer."

"Wait—we'll fix Annie in, like we do on the swing."

They take Annie's scarf, which she isn't wearing but which she's brought in case it turns colder, and they tie it around her waist to the chair frame. Then they take hold of the handle and pull the chair up the slope a little, only a few steps.

Then they turn and say:

"Ready! Here we go!"

And they run the few steps down the slope, pushing Annie ahead of them. It is not very fast, but Annie begs them to do it again.

They go back, a little farther up this time.

Down they go and as they run down, Annie throws her head back and squeals.

"Again!" she says. "Again! Again!"

They do it over and over again. Up the slope, down they go, faster and faster and then slowing down as they go up the other side. Annie's fair hair streams out behind her as if the wind was blowing it and each time she squeals louder and louder, as if by squealing she could show them her joy, her marvelous joy, at flying through the air. In a wheel chair. Ben is excited and feels happy because she is happy and it is they, Steve and Ben, making her happy.

"Once more, once more!" cries Annie. "Please, please."

So, they pull her up once more, one last time, and turn and start down the slope, Annie's hair flying, Annie's squeals and cries flying through the air and Ben and Steve's feet pounding on the grass, holding the flying wheel chair steady.

Then the nightmare starts. A great red hand comes down on the handle with a thump and Ben sees it and wonders what it is and before he can think another thing, a slashing blow on the side of his head sends him flying. Annie, he thinks, Annie, she'll crash if I let go, but Ben is too far away from the chair now, oh, Steve hang on, hang on. But Ben has got it all wrong, because as he lies there, his head spinning, he sees the wheel chair standing still and all he hears is a stream of words hammering into his ears.

"Crazy little beasts, you, what d'you think

you're doing? Must be mad. Fools, idiots, are you out of your minds? Torturing a kid like that. Making her scream. A kid like *that*, too. Trapped in that thing. Can't hit back. Bastards! Murderers! Hooligans! I could . . ."

The words shower down over Ben and he doesn't know what it's all about. He looks up from where he's fallen and sees a large man holding Annie's chair and Steve is on the ground, too, holding his ear. The man is furiously angry and kicks out at Steve again, shouting:

"What've you got to say, eh? Go on, speak up! I caught you! I caught you red-handed. Now try and get out of it."

Annie is sitting quite still, looking frightened, tears beginning to run down her face.

Ben gets up slowly and feels dizzy.

"What's your name?" says the man.

"Ben," says Ben.

"And yours?" he says to Steve.

"Steve," says Steve, trying not to cry.

"And where do you live?"

Ben tells him.

"Well, I'm going right back there now,

and you're coming with me. And I'm telling
your parents what you've been up to. And I
hope they tell the police. Never seen anything
like it. A child like that. A poor crippled
child and helpless and you two torturing her,
making her scream, making her cry. Locked
up, that's what you two ought to be. Flogged,
that's it."

Ben tries to explain.

"But we—"

But the man clouts him over the ear with his fist.

"Shut your filthy little mouth now. I saw you."

Steve blurts out: "She likes it. She likes it. We did it for her . . . didn't we, Annie?"

Annie's small face is crumpled and she is staring at the man, her eyes wide open, her hands shaking, her whole self shaking. Ben sees she is frightened and her whole world has fallen to pieces.

"Mmmmm," she says, the tears falling.

"See!" shouts the man, his mouth red and angry. "See, she's scared stiff. You've scared the daylights out of her."

And he grips the handle of the chair and grabs Ben by the top of his arm and marches off, telling Steve to follow. They walk away, Ben and Steve too numb to say or do anything, and they walk across the city, all the way, until they get to Ben's street, and there's Annie's mother coming toward them. She's been watching from the window, and when she sees Annie coming and a strange man pushing her chair, she rushes straight down the steps and along the pavement to meet them.

"What is it?" she says. "Is she hurt? Is she all right?"

"She's all right, missis," says the man. "She's all right. I've brought these two back, so you'll know the truth."

And it gets worse and worse. When Annie's mother hears what they've been doing, she screams and screams and says how could he, he, Ben, whom she trusted Annie with? And she shouts at Steve and tells him to get on away home. And Ben is left alone with them, and Annie's dad shouts at him too, and Annie sits there, quiet as quiet, her eyes staring, at Ben, at her mother, at her father, at the strange man who came and spoiled their marvelous game when she flew like a bird through the air and let the wind whistle through her hair. She knows she'll never play the game again.

Annie's dad goes storming up the stairs, dragging Ben after him and banging like thunder on the door, and when Mother opens up, he pushes straight past her and shakes Ben like a dog shaking a rat.

"Where's your room, now? Just tell me and no lip, thank you." And Ben points and Annie's dad goes straight in there and rips out the tick-tock box and all the wires and smashes the whole lot down onto the floor. Then he picks up the wreckage and stamps out of the apartment with one last shout.

"And don't let me ever hear you speaking to our Annie again," he yells from the top of the stairs. "Ever, ever again." And then he goes down the stairs.

And Mother cries: "What's all this? What's going on? Tell me, Ben. What's the matter with them all? What's happened?"

But Ben can't say a single thing. Not a word comes out of his mouth and his stomach has curled up and his whole brain has stopped working with the shock of what Annie's dad has done and what they all think, all of them. And they never stop to ask what really happened. They never stop to ask Annie about what it's like flying through the air, about the wind in your ears, what it's like being a bird on a clothesline, of the joy of it all, of the squealing marvelous happiness of it all. They never stop to ask. Ben goes into his room and sits down on his bed and slowly the tears come up into his throat and he tries to push them down again, punching his pillow, punching his bed, punching his fist on his knees, on his other hand, punching and punching and punching at them all, because they don't know anything at all, any of them.

JOAN TATE lives in Shrewsbury, England, and spends her working time reading for publishers, translating, and writing her own books.

She has written a great number of stories and books for children of all ages.